Th

A Pa

Leti Diaz

****

Diaz, Leti

The Wild Rosebush: A Parable of Unforgiveness / written by Leti Diaz

ISBN: 978-1-945526-74.9

Library of Congress Control Number: 2019910565

Printed in the United States of America

I Street Press
828 I Street
Sacramento, CA 95814

I dedicate this book to my Lord Jesus Christ who called me out of that dark place of unforgiveness to rule and reign with Him in love, joy, and peace.

Acknowledgements

I would like to thank my sisters in Christ, especially Bridget Wedgeworth, Ana Mendez, and Anita Melville who encouraged me to keep going when the going was tough. Bridget, thank you for opening your beautiful, peaceful home for us to get together and write, and for your encouraging words and dream interpretations. And for Joan Stabe who helped edit this book; I couldn't have done it without you, what a gift! And thanks to my prayer partners who took time to pray this book through. And last but not least, Pastor Joel Pappas, who has walked with me through my healing journey.

Introduction

Wow, who would have thought I'd come this far? I'm now set free and walking the walk God planned out for me. I've embraced who I am; I am no longer worrying about what other people think of me. I've met and have wonderful people around me that encourage and walk alongside me; they are awesome.

Many people saw me as put together, happy and care free. Some saw me as needing a little "help", but I knew who I was; I was a guarded woman, mostly quiet, sometimes a bit abrasive and fairly intelligent. Behind all that was a very hurt and discouraged woman, with deep wounds, unforgiving with some folks and with walls to keep others out; it was self-preservation. I functioned as best I could. Sometimes I pretended I was happy and had it all together, but mostly I was just coping. I'm now happy, enjoying life, and most of all free.

Growing up, I felt lots of disappointments; I had friends and family who I thought were friends and found out they were talking about me behind my back. I didn't feel confident enough to ask my parents for things I needed. There were so many things I can list, but I'd rather spend time sharing about my rosebush experience. My dreams were crushed and whirled around me like a wave from the ocean, twirling me around in lies of deception.

Deception, lies and lack of trust can sometimes sabotage the choices we make; they can keep us bound and unable to walk freely in who we are. When I thought that things were going my way and suddenly the bottom fell out, I was left alone wondering what in the world I did wrong. Why did God allow the circumstance to happen in the first place? A whirlwind of disappointment brought back those horrible memories and stopped me in my tracks yet again.

Helpless? No. Forgotten? No. Loved? Yes.

Have you hardened your heart? Are there recurring memories you keep reliving over and over again, that just won't stop?

Have you forgiven the person, or the people that hurt you?

Have you forgiven God?

Most importantly…

Have you forgiven yourself?

Unforgiveness keeps you bound and connected to the person, people or situations that wounded you. It's like a ball and chain you carry around with you everywhere you go. It's like a dark cloud that hovers over you night and day, day and night; there's no escaping it. You are being controlled by the memories and lies, and you're allowing them to hurt you all over again; you are actually reliving what those memories and lies did to you. You think you're in control and think you have the abusers and users in the palm of your hand by not forgiving them, but in reality, by not forgiving, who's holding who?

Forgiveness is one of the keys that releases you from all that anguish, pain and suffering. Forgiveness is like a breath of fresh air that will take you to that place of joy, to that place of peace, to that place of rest, and to that place of freedom. That place of forgiveness will lift you up into the freedom that you are so desperately seeking.

There *IS FREEDOM* from what has kept you bound, Freedom of the memories, Freedom to finally let go, Freedom to live again, Freedom to love again, Freedom to laugh again, Freedom to be you, Freedom to be that beautiful innocent fun-loving person God created – YOU!

Each person has their own way of dealing with things. I'm not saying that what I experienced will help you the way it helped me, but I'm hoping to give you a glimpse of how the Lord helped me to truly, finally let go and forgive. The Lord shows me things by analogy or parables; I've applied what's in the Bible by what I have and am experiencing in life.

One of the most important things I have learned is that forgiveness is paramount; it's the most valuable and most important lesson we will ever learn if we are to live a happy and joyous life.

In Matthew 6:14-15 (NKJV) ("The Lord's Prayer"), Jesus teaches about forgiveness, "For if you forgive men their trespasses, your heavenly Father will also forgive you. But if you do not forgive men their trespasses, neither will your Father forgive your trespasses."

Wow, really, I'm supposed to forgive those people for what they did to me!? Wait a minute! They're the ones that violated me; they're the ones that hurt me, lied to me, stole from me, took everything I had; they damaged my soul… and I'm supposed to forgive them!?

Obedience is better than sacrifice as stated in [(1)]1 Samuel 15:22 (NKJV), "…Behold, to obey is better than sacrifice..." Ok, I'll take that first step. Alright! I'll forgive! It won't be easy, but I'll do it! I'll obey God, and I'll let Him take me through the difficult journey of forgiveness no matter how long it takes for it to reach my heart.

Yes, I said it not only once, twice or even 10 times; I've done it for years. Okay Lord, can you hear me!? I forgive them for what they said and did to me. I forgave them alright, but it was just in my head not in my heart where it really mattered. I really needed it to get from my head to my heart. I needed it to be "real", a true forgiveness, not just empty words, but life-giving words of forgiveness! Forgiveness sometimes isn't very easy to do, but it's something we must do if we want to live free, live happy, and live loved.

Again, it wasn't easy, but I did it! The Lord finally softened my heart enough to finally let forgiveness sink into my heart, into my inner most being, down deep into my soul and to let go of the past abuses, hurts and disappointments. And instead of letting unforgiveness rule my life, I let Jesus in; He now lives in my heart where I now have the peace and reassurance that the painful memories will no longer rule over me. The Lord taught me that if I don't forgive, my anger will grow into more roots of bitterness, anger, hatred, and resentment. It will intertwine itself in everything I do and how I see things and say things. It will spill over and affect the people that I love and the innocent people around me.

You know, every once in a while, I would think of the "*Rosebush Encounter*" to remind myself that Jesus was standing right there with me, ministering to my soul as I was digging and travailing over the ground of past hurtful memories. He was there helping me to uproot all the bitterness, anger, hatred, loneliness, fear, sadness and disappointments that I had masked under a veil of contentment so others wouldn't see my pain. I was tired of pretending to be strong; thank you Lord for helping me to forgive and for setting me free!

Once all the unforgiveness was uprooted, He reminded me to be careful not to pick them back up again otherwise I'd be right back where I started, letting those people hurt me all over again. I was set free by giving all those hurts to Him, Jesus. You see, the enemy will try to reseed those old hurts and wounds back into your thought life, back into your heart and invade your beautiful garden of peace. Be careful to guard your heart at all times and in all situations; remember there's a reward for those that forgive…it's called FREEDOM.

I hope you enjoy this story, and my biggest hope is that the analogy/parable the Lord showed me helps you too!

May the Lord give you strength to let go and forgive.

Leti

The Wild Rosebush

My two young daughters and I uprooted ourselves from San Jose, CA to move to Sacramento, CA, not only for a new job that I interviewed for and received, but mostly to get away from the place of hurtful memories; I wanted a fresh start.

It wasn't an easy move. I moved to a place that was unfamiliar to me and where I didn't know anyone. I was running away from my past, hoping it would be easier to rid myself of the hurtful memories that were so deeply rooted in my heart. I was running away from the thoughts, remembrances, disappointments, and betrayal that haunted me every day of my life. No matter how or what I tried, or who I dated nothing made me happy. All I could think of was to run away; I was running to safety, running to a place where no one knew me, running to a new beginning.

But that move came with a high price. My girls ended up being latchkey kids for a while, something I thought would never happen. That move isolated not only me but my girls as well. I was lonelier than I had ever been, and I robbed my girls of the relationships they once had with their cousins, aunts, uncles, grandparents and friends. I took away their familiar and comfortable places; I took away their comfort zone and their safety net. I robbed them of their fun, joy, peace, and trust. The consequences of me running away cost my girls dearly. I believe it caused them to shut down and not trust so easily. Although I was there for them, I felt that it caused an invincible wedge between us. I now know they felt abandoned. My hurt, hurt them.

"Lord, may they forgive me for taking them away from their place of security and the place they loved. And Lord, I forgive myself for the guilt of taking them away from the people they loved and trusted."

We eventually bought a home that had a huge backyard with lots of fruit trees and grape vines. There was an apple, plum, peach, nectarine, apricot, and an orange tree. There were also a few "wild" rosebushes and of course decorative hedges. But one thing I noticed near the back fence, just two feet away from each other, on the left, was an orange tree, and on the right was a wild rosebush. I thought to myself, "Why in the world did the previous owner plant them so close together? That made no sense." Well, come to find out, roses are planted near grapevines as an early disease detection warning system. If there's disease on the rosebush leaves then it's time to take action to protect the surrounding trees and plants. Rosebushes also attract bees which help with pollination. Okay, now it makes sense. But still, I wanted to remove them. They were pretty but messy at the same time, and they would get entangled in everything that was in their path. (*Like our unforgiveness*)

During the summer the grapevines and wild rosebushes grew incredibly fast, and both would intertwine with each other. Picture this, starting from left to right, there was an orange tree, a grapevine in the middle and a wild rosebush on the right. On the left, you have the grapevines intertwining with the orange tree; on the right you have the rosebush and grapevines intertwining with each other.

Each year I would have to try and gently remove the grapevines from the orange tree and wild rosebushes. Both the orange tree and wild rosebushes had thorns so they needed to be separated so that the grape leaves wouldn't get cut by the thorny stems and catch a disease. Each year I would get scratched and cut by those gnarly thorns. (Here we go with the memories! The thorns represented the memories which were hurting me again.) I finally got tired of this ritual of having to spend my precious time untangling that mess. Plus, I didn't want to spend time "gardening" more than I had to; I wanted to spend more time with my girls. This was the year to take action, but it was too hot in the summer to remove the bushes. So, the long four-day winter holiday weekend was when I'd do this. The plants and trees were in the dormant stage and the ground wasn't too hard.

I'll miss those beautiful roses; they were lovely to look at when they were in full bloom. But like in life, we sometimes have to get rid of or leave the place we are so familiar with. We need to get away from the poisonous atmosphere and toxic people that are trying to hold us back. It isn't easy. I left behind all that was familiar to me. Where was God leading me? What was His plan for my life, for our lives?

Well, the day finally came, the four-day weekend; it was a bit foggy when I started. The air was crisp, cold with a slight breeze, and amazingly it warmed up a bit in the afternoon; it was perfect weather to "get it done". I started in on the digging late that Friday morning, I had mowed the lawn, pruned the grapevines and other plants in the yard. I thought it was going to be a one, two, three it's a done deal. Boy was I wrong! It took me two long exhausting days just to dig out those rosebushes; it turned out to be more than one bush, with a few surprises.

The rosebushes were not in bloom, thank goodness! Otherwise it would have been hard to remove what I was so used to seeing for years, beautiful pink blossoms.

Plus, I noticed the rosebushes were "diseased", and they needed to come out. Was I having second thoughts? Did I really want to get rid of them, or should I keep them? (Yes, I needed freedom.) I started with the smaller rosebush. First, I clipped more stems to make a path to where I was going to start digging. I started near the base of the bush, and since it had rained a few weeks prior, the ground was soft and easy to dig.

The ground may have been soft, but the root was deep, and I had to be careful not to accidentally cut the sprinkler line that was running parallel with the root system. I dug until I finally found the main root. "That only took a few long hours," I thought to myself as I shook my head.

To my surprise, as I started to yank the trunk with its root, it wouldn't come up; it didn't want to yield to my tugging. I dug around the trunk a little more, and as I did, it revealed another root, which uncovered the reason it didn't come up the first time. It was a huge root ball. I did not realize that the wild rosebush had these huge roots balls, I thought it was "just roots". I severed that root, yanked twice and most of it came up. And what do you think I saw? Yes, another root was attached to the large root, but this very long root led to a different rosebush about seven feet away. I had no clue they were all connected. The look on my face was total shock, gasping and thinking, "Oh no, more work!" That other rosebush also needed to go. I knew I had more work in front of me. Are you tired yet? I was…

Roots, roots and more roots were causing more entanglements. (My unforgiveness was causing more roots of anger and resentment, and it was being entangled in all areas of my life.)

Yay, I dug up my first rosebush; my face was sweaty and dirty. I had accomplished what I had set out to do. Then came the disappointment. I realized that there was no one there to see my accomplishment, no one to see what I had been doing all morning and afternoon, toiling over this one bush. I brushed off that thought, and as proud as I could be, I took hold of that trunk and large root and held it up. I held it up high like a trophy, like an athlete that had just finished a long arduous race. The perspiration was running down my face, my clothes covered with sweat and dirt. How exhilarating! The applause in my head was so loud and clear; I could hear people cheering me on, clapping and yelling, "Yay, you did it; you did it; you crossed the finish line, you got rid of the roots!" Then with a blink of an eye, it was over; the applause stopped and the people faded away. I let down my arms and tossed that trunk, large root and all in the pile of already cut stems which were piled high on the lawn. Then, I thought to myself, "OKAY, back to reality, one out, one more to go." I then had to focus and prepare myself for the next "race".

The first wild rosebush was the smaller of the two, which, of course, was the easiest to dig out. It was ridiculously exhausting!

I began to dig around the next bush. I thought it was going to be easy, but that stubborn root proved to be a bit harder than I had anticipated. I just wanted it to be done; I was tired and getting sore. I knew I had more work in front of me. I wanted that root to let go of its hold in the ground. What an image! *That root was holding onto the ground and I was holding on to that unforgiveness!* Stubbornness and not wanting to let go of what I had held on to for so long was what I was accustomed to. What would I do with myself or how would I feel after I let go? Would I have to fill in that empty space with something else? Something that was unfamiliar to me, like "***Love*** and ***Acceptance***"? What else could it be? How about peace and/or joy? No, wait! I got it! FREEDOM! Yes, freedom from all the roots of anger, hatred, bitterness, resentment, disappointments and rejection. But what is that going to feel like? That was new territory that I was not only willing to face, but to accept.

I wanted to be me! Happy, loving, giving, loyal and free; that's my true identity. A person's past does not define who they are!

I hadn't done that much exercise in a very long time, and my body wasn't used to what I was putting it through. My back, my arms, my legs, my shoulders, and neck were taking a toll. I was in a bit of pain. "Oh my," I thought to myself, "I should have paid someone to do this for me!" But sometimes you have to be willing to go the extra mile and travail through the pain.

I had to take a break! I was already tired from the yardwork and digging that I had done earlier in the day. It was probably around 2:00 p.m. I was beat and hungry, so I decided to have lunch. I cleaned myself up as best I could and headed to the kitchen, grabbed lunch, took it outside and ate by the place I had been digging. I stood there with my lunch and leaned against the shovel and went into lala dream land. I was playing a scene in my mind of just resting and relaxing in my beach chair with a cup of hot coffee and looking out into the ocean. I could hear the waves crashing on the shore as I watched the seagulls fly by and felt the cool breeze on my face. Ahhh how refreshing! A few minutes later that bubble burst, poof all gone, so I finished my lunch and went back to the grinding stone, time to continue.

I didn't realize how much work it was to dig, pick up dirt and toss, dig, pick up dirt, and toss, over and over again. But I was definitely determined, excited and proud of myself at this point. I was getting it done! I'm not one that easily gives up; I have to finish the task at hand.

Now to continue with the second rosebush: I took a deep breath and had one last glimpse of my beautiful ocean dream. Once I shook that off, I picked up the shovel and began to dig again… dig, pick up dirt and toss, dig, pick up dirt and toss, etc. etc. My goal, of course, at this time was to get to the "root of this problem". (Ha-ha, just a quick pun.)

I dug and dug and dug. I was at half foot deep, then another half foot, seriously…. arghhh and still the trunk was hidden deep in the dirt.

At this point, I had to take another break! I again rested myself on the handle of the shovel, wiped the sweat off my brow, took a drink of water and started the process all over again.

I was at the point of giving up; my shoulders and back were yelling at me to stop, but I knew I was almost there. I really didn't want to give up! I looked past my pain and frustration and sore muscles and began to dig a little more. Then there it was, a root, a small one. So, I dug around it; then I bent down to tug at it to see where I had to continue digging. Then finally, another root appeared, a very thick one. Excited, I grabbed the shovel and with one big downward motion I was able to slice the end of that root that was holding it in the ground. Then I pulled again thinking, "Yay!! I'm done!" But to my utter disbelief, there was another thick root holding it down on the opposite side. I was more than flabbergasted; I was angry, so angry I wanted to scream! I wanted to finish! I was tired…. I was exhausted… I threw down the shovel and stomped away wanting to get away from what was making me so angry and frustrated. Like so many other times, I wanted to run away from my problems. After a few minutes of resting, contemplating what to do next, and not wanting to give up, I headed back to begin the process all over again, but this time positioned myself on the other side of the rosebush where that big thick root was.

I dug, and I pulled, and I dug some more and voila! I saw the other side of the root. I sliced this one as well, again thinking that was it. Nope! I stomped my foot, tossed the shovel away from me as far as I could and threw my arms to my side. There was another *dang* root holding down this big ball. It was almost as thick as the rosebush trunk above the ground. My head was spinning at this point! It's going to take me at least another hour or two to get that root completely out. There were more than three roots holding down this one rosebush… I had to stop! There was no way I could go on; I was too exhausted! Feeling defeated, I went inside, took a shower, took some pain meds, made dinner for my girls and myself, cleaned up after dinner and went straight to bed.

I woke up thinking, "Today is another day. I wish my brother was here to help me." He was a landscaper after all, but he lived more than two hours away, and was a busy man taking care of his own family. But I should have asked him or paid someone to do it!!!

Here I am! I'm back, and I'm not going to let this "little" problem defeat me. I'm going to wrestle through it. After resting and clearing my mind of yesterday's battle, I took another look at the area I had dug and noticed that the root was not only deep, but its roots extended sideways out about six feet. It too was thick! I came to the resolve that I had no choice but to continue. I'm a fighter and was determined that nothing was going to get in my way. I thought to myself, "I'm going to defeat this giant!" Same as yesterday, dig, pick up dirt and toss, dig, pick up dirt and toss. I finally got to the root, it was about 12" in diameter, it was huge, so I dug, and I dug and gave it one good pull and out it came!

I stood there for a second in sheer exhaustion and excitement thanking God. I started singing my halleluiahs at the top of my lungs and dancing in circles like a mad woman. It was finally over!

I was so excited, I had to show my girls! I picked up this heavy root; it looked like a small pumpkin. I walked over to the big living room window, my heart pounding, I was covered in dirt and sweat and smiling ear to ear. I started tapping on the glass to get their attention. No one came, so I tapped a little harder! I don't know how many times I had to tap, then finally! They came around the corner. I showed them that humongous root (my second trophy) and to my shock filled face and surprise… all they did was smile and nodded with approval, then they looked at each other, shrugged their shoulders, looked at me again, smiled and walked away. What no applause for your mother's hard work? Gees, kids these days; I tell ya! They obviously were not as exuberantly excited as I was; they weren't even excited. Hey, I was excited. This was a huge achievement. I didn't give up. At least yesterday I had a whole crowd cheering me on… I just sighed, turned around, and walked back towards the area where I was digging and gladly tossed that monster onto the already existing pile of cut stems and thorny, ugly, hurtful branches. Then I began to fill that empty hole with dirt. As I was doing this, the Lord began to speak to my heart. I considered what He was sharing, and I embraced what He revealed to me.

The first wild rosebush was the smaller of the two bushes, which, of course, was the easiest to dig out, even though it was an exhausting task.

Here's the revelation…

A lot of people have hurts, anger, disappointments and resentments that they hold on to, and some may have been hidden for years. Some of these thoughts and situations have grown poisonous roots in our hearts. Some roots are small; some are large. The bigger the root, the harder it is to get rid of, or in this case, dig out. Small roots are easier to get rid of. You might hold on to the roots of offense for a few days, a few weeks, then you finally make up your mind and say, "Okay, I forgive you for what you have done or said." The "root" is then taken care of; it's been removed and all it took was a moment. It just took a quick decision to say, "I forgive you." The offensive root didn't have time to grow any bigger.

But if the bigger roots that created the hurts and disappointments are deep, it may take years and years to get rid of them. We want to forgive, but sometimes the memories or thoughts come back, and we bury them again; we've allowed that root to grow, get thicker, and deeper. Finally, years and years later, we ask God, we plead with God, "Lord, please take this pain and hurt from me. I don't want them anymore, please help me to forgive!"

There were times when I tried to forgive the offenses, but failed. I'd forgive; then the anger, bitterness, hatred and resentments were there again.

You see, God already made a way to get rid of that unforgiveness. Here are a few examples, (1)Matthew 6:12 (NKJV), "And forgive us our debts, as we forgive our debtors." Or how about (1)Matthew 6:15 (NKJV), "But if you do not forgive men their trespasses, neither will your Father forgive your trespasses."

In order for you to be free of any offense and to stop others from hurting you again, you need to free the other person. Release that person by forgiving them. Doing this will help stop the sting of what they did to you. We can't just ignore what God is trying to tell us; His words are there to help you and me. Even Jesus forgave those who nailed Him to the cross; He said, "...Father, forgive them, for they do not know what they do." (1)Luke 23:34 (NKJV).

The Lord tugs and tugs at those roots in our hearts because He wants us to be free. He wants us to let go of those offenses and those hurts. Here we are handing it to Him, but then without a thought we often take it right back.

Are you ready to be set free? Will you let it go and give it to Him? Will you take that chance? Will you give Him that small root that was never dealt with or will you say, "Nah, I'll leave it there, no need to forgive; it'll die; it's not a big deal. I'll just forget about it?" If so, that small piece that was left can get nourished by its surroundings. For example, people telling you, "I wouldn't have forgiven them," or "That person is no good", or "They're not worth forgiving", etc. And there you have it, you've allowed that small root to grow into another "large root" that you'll have to dig up and spend unnecessary time on. Do you really want to travail on hard ground again? Don't let the past define who you are or allow others to deter you from doing the right thing, forgive. Spend a little more time forgiving and releasing the hurts and disappointments right away. It'll be worth it! And you'll feel free and cleansed!

It may not be easy to let go; you may need to relive those memories. It could be a little scary having to open up that wound again, not knowing what will come next. But, will you do it?

Some of the roots/memories were hurtful, and some were agonizingly painful, and some didn't hurt as bad as you thought they would. It all depends on the situations. But, in order to heal you will need to take, perhaps many, first steps and forgive.

I was afraid to forgive, not knowing what might happen next and afraid that that person was going to hurt me again. I shouldn't have been afraid to forgive because all I was doing by not forgiving was hurting myself emotionally. I was reliving the past over and over again. The past was a stumbling block, not allowing me to grow into who I was meant to be, a person I truly believed I could be, a person filled with peace, love, patience, and joy, a person ready to go out and trust and love people again.

Once I knew that I had truly forgiven those that hurt me, all that bitterness, anger, and resentment left. But what was left behind was a big empty hole in my heart, and I knew that hole needed to get filled. I decided right then to fill it with God's love, His peace, His grace and most importantly His forgiveness. Peace and freedom are what I longed for, and I finally received it by forgiving everyone that hurt me. "I'm free to be me!" I'm so very happy now. Life isn't perfect, but struggles don't affect me like they used to. I see problems and disappointments differently. It's easier to forgive, and actually, I don't harbor or hold on to negative feelings now that I've learned to forgive. It no longer affects me like it used to. I'm free; I'm accepted by the Beloved. God loves me just as I am.

FREEEDOOOMMM!

I prayed, "Lord, I forgive (name) for what was said and done to me. I release all the anger, bitterness, resentments, disappointments and fear. And instead of the anger, Lord, fill me with love. Instead of the bitterness, Lord, fill me with forgiveness. Instead of resentment, Lord, fill me with acceptance. Instead of the disappointment,

Lord, fill me with expectancy. And instead of fear, Lord, fill me with faith. Amen." (Feel free to use this same prayer.)

I'm so thankful that God still speaks to us today. He used a gnarly, unkempt rosebush to show me the beauty (the rose, the outer shell, the bloom) to see what was hidden underneath the rose which were the struggles, the twisted lies, anger, and the deceptions that were keeping me bound within its thorns. He also showed me the laughter, joy and freedom that could be achieved once I chose to rid myself of all the unforgiveness and lies that held me bound for so long.

The work and exhaustion which I undertook was the lesson of the struggle and stubbornness of waiting so long to forgive. As a result, I had no choice but to wait to receive that joy, peace and freedom I so longed for. The applause and holding that root like a trophy is a symbolic view of the triumph and freedom I so longed for. I ran the race, won, and I finally let it go.

It's time to get rid of those "roots" and be set free forever.

FORGIVE and LIVE again!

There's so much out there; there's so much to live for. Look around you, see the beauty, and then, "Stop and smell the roses."

Food for thought: In the beginning of the book I wrote:

Helpless? No. Forgotten? No. Loved? Yes.

What lesson can you learn from your past experience/experiences? Have you hardened your heart? Have you relived that awful thing that has happened to you over and over again, and just won't stop? Have you forgiven the person or the people that hurt you? Have you forgiven God, but most importantly, have you forgiven yourself? How about establishing "good" roots, roots that will blossom into a stunning rosebush that creates blossoms of beautifully fragrant perfume that people want to be around?

Let's be imitators of Christ; love one another, be at peace with one another, preferring one another. Let's be the world changers, taking what was meant for evil and hate and turning it around for good, making it lovely, loveable, and joyful. Forgive others, forgive yourself.

In [1]Ephesians 4:31-32 (NKJV), we read: "Let all bitterness, wrath, anger, clamor, and evil speaking be put away from you, with all malice. And be kind to one another, tenderhearted, forgiving one another, just as God in Christ forgave you."

Note: I'm not a psychologist or counselor; I'm a woman like any other who has gone through some hard times and disappointments in her life and the Lord helped me through them ALL. Hearing His still quiet voice, and reading His Word, the Bible with its parables helped me as well. If we listen, He'll direct us in the right direction to freedom. Let Him direct you.

He also used psychologists, counselors, pastors and friends to help me conquer the demons in my life. But if you're battling something that is so deep you can't deal with on your own, I would highly recommend Christian counseling. It's helped me!

Meaning of:

[2](Merriam Webster Dictionary, Since 1828)

Unforgiveness:	Unforgiving- Unwilling or unable to forgive. Holding a grudge against someone.
Anger:	A strong feeling of displeasure
Rage:	Violent and uncontrolled anger, a fit of violent wrath
Wrath:	Strong vengeful anger or indignation
Bitterness:	Marked by intensity or severity: a: accompanied by severe pain or suffering b: determined: VEHEMENT c: exhibiting intense animosity d (1): harshly reproachful (2): marked by cynicism and chosen Caused by or expressive of severe pain, grief, or regret
Hatred:	Extreme dislike or disgust: HATE. Ill will or resentment that is usually mutual: prejudiced hostility or animosity

Unforgiveness can come in many ways:

A hurtful word	Cheating spouse
Abuse in all its forms	Broken promises
Needs not being met	Favoritism
False expectations	Unresolved anger
Jealousy	Resentment
Arguments	Backbiting
Gossip	Disappointment
Stolen ideas	Abandonment
You fill in the blanks	

- Have you forgiven yourself?
- Are there some things that were said and done to you that you think can't be forgiven?
- Have you believed the lie that you cannot be forgiven?

Have you:

- Lied
- Harbored anger towards God
- Stolen
- Committed murder
- Spoken or thought evil thoughts
- Cheated on your spouse (physically or in your thoughts)
- Held onto the past
- Manipulated others
- Embraced a wrong lifestyle
- Had an abortion
- Regretted not doing something you should have done and lost an opportunity
- Etc.

All the items listed above can all be forgiven; simply ask the Lord to forgive you. And He will.

Before I continue, I'd like to say, which I think is important, and it took me awhile to sort this one out, is… just because you forgive someone doesn't mean you have to be in their circle of influence. You don't have to talk to or see them again, no matter who they are. There's no guilt or shame in that. Be free!

♥

- Here are some questions that can dig out some of those roots.

- Be honest with yourself; write down exactly how you feel, give it to the Lord, simply forgive. Take accountability for your actions.

- When writing, please don't be limited to the space given below. Grab another piece of paper or a notebook. There are also a few blank pages in the back of the book for your convenience. Write as much as you can. Let it all go. Write down every detail of your experience. Once you're done, you can rip it up or keep it, whichever helps you to "let go".

1. Who do you need to forgive and why?

2. If you cannot forgive, write down why you can't or won't forgive?

3. Have you hardened your heart? If yes, why?

4. What lesson can you learn from your past experience/experiences?

5. Have you relived that awful thing that has happened to you over and over again? What is it that you're reliving?

6. Are you blaming others for your unforgiveness instead of taking responsibility for your own attitude/actions?

7. Have you forgiven God? If not, why?

8. But most importantly, have you forgiven yourself? If not, why?

There are probably other questions you can ask or other scenarios you can consider that I didn't list. Go with the flow. Ask the Lord to help you through the journey of forgiving. Don't limit God; be opened minded and be willing to take the first step to an incredible journey of what the Lord has in store for you.

There are some places you won't want to return to that are hurtful and scary. If that's the case, don't go it alone; seek outside help with either a pastor, therapist, counselor, doctor, or friend; find someone you trust and begin your healing journey. Be free.

What are the next steps in your journey?

1. ______________________________

2. ______________________________

3. ______________________________

4. ______________________________

5. ______________________________

Don't let unforgiveness rule your life; start living a life of freedom and joy!

♥

"Therefore, if the Son makes you free, you shall be free indeed."

[1]John 8:36 (NKJV)

Bibliography

(1) Scripture taken from the New King James Version®. Copyright © 1982 by Thomas Nelson.

(2) Merriam Webster Dictionary, Merriam Webster, Incorporated, Springfield, MA. 2019 https://www.merriam-webster.com

About the Author

Leti Diaz is an ordained minister, conference speaker, and author with a heart for women who need encouragement, hope and love. Her desire is to see women set free from past hurts and disappointments. She's a graduate of International College of Bible Theology, Missouri, with a Bachelor's degree in Biblical Studies. She's a Radio Producer, a team member of Life Teams International, and a Women's Ministry Leader. Leti has ministered in Los Angeles, Salinas, Sacramento, and Mexico. She also writes poetry, likes to paint, sing and travel. She's a mother of two amazing daughters, and grandmother to four beautiful grandchildren.

Notes

Notes

Made in the USA
Columbia, SC
23 November 2024